SUMO CITY

By Keith M. Duncan

ISBN: 9798484313662

First edition 2021

Text, Cover Design & Illustrations
Keith M Duncan

Graphics & Layout
Mark Schlesinger
(Print Team, Norwich)

Printed and Distributed by
Kindle Direct Publishing, an Amazon Company

Published by
K M Duncan

SumoCat

By Keith M. Duncan

This book is dedicated to a beloved pet
Seaweed

ILLUSTRATIONS

CONTENTS

INTRODUCTION

by the Author

Welcome to the world of SumoCat.

A creation that came about from the antics of my own pets Sid, Daisy and Poppy. In particular the one that inspired the lead character. Sid spends much of his time rolling about on the driveway, sleeping on his back and most importantly eating. Whilst watching this rather large cat making a bit of a performance of cleaning his back, both my neighbour and I agreed that he looked very much like a Sumo Wrestler going about some ritualistic moves before a match.

I immediately put pen to paper and drew a cartoon of Sid wearing a mawashi (a Sumo Wrestler's loincloth). This gave rise to putting together a story set loosely in Sid's real home environment, to include illustrations.

The story follows the adventures of a very large domestic cat that lives with his two cat companions and his two human domestics, in a small cottage in North Norfolk. After a night of high winds he makes a discovery in an old upturned wheelie bin, which will change his life forever, and provide a great deal of fun and entertainment for him and his friends.

The book has nine short chapters and takes the reader through a series of illustrated adventures as SumoCat finds himself in all sorts of un-expected situations and facing new challenges. It is aimed at children mainly but parents and guardians may also find the content humorous and entertaining. It is also intended as an educational tool with it's many references. A child may well ask what is meant by certain words or turns of phrase. This is intentional and will give a parent or guardian the opportunity of providing the answers.

This publication has been produced as a prelude to further stories following the many adventures of SumoCat.

Chapter One
The Sunday Magazine

It was a warm sunny morning in the village of Little Souls, and one little soul had not slept very well due to a very windy night making the cat flap sound as if there was an army of cat visitors coming into the house. Sid found this extremely disturbing as he was a gentle and quiet living cat and took his leisure very seriously. His two cat companions Daisy and Poppy had managed to sleep through all the noise and the two human domestics who shared the cottage with them were also still in bed.

Sid decided it was time to inspect the damage that the wind had caused and squeezed through the cat flap to go and have a look. This was a bit of a task as Sid was a rather large cat, in fact on his very occasional visits to the vets and the cattery he would travel in a medium size dog box.

Once in the garden of Pear Tree Cottage, which was his home, he noticed that the big green recycling waste bin had fallen over. As curiosity got the better of him he decided to go and inspect its contents, which were now spread untidily on the driveway.

There were a few plastic bottles, some old newspapers, and a couple of empty cat biscuit boxes, which Sid checked had not been thrown away too soon. He then noticed a very colourful glossy magazine that had fallen out of one of the newspapers. Upon closer inspection he could see that on one of the pages, that had flopped open, there was a picture of a very large man squatting opposite another large man wearing a big towel around his middle. In fact both men were wearing towels and looked very much as though they were about to have a fight.

At this point Daisy who had just woken up came along and saw what Sid was up to. Poor little Daisy wore an eye patch because she had hurt her eye in an accident, but being a self-educated cat, she could still read, and told Sid that the two men in the picture were Sumo Wrestlers. Sid thought to himself that this looked like a fun thing to do and asked Daisy to read all there was to read in the magazine about the Sumo Wrestlers. He liked the way they looked and rather fancied having a go himself. It could be a way of making some new friends who he could tumble around and have play fights with. Seeing that Sid was so keen, Daisy explained to him that the loin cloth that a Sumo wrestler wears is called a 'mawashi 'and the name of a wrestler in Japanese is a 'rikishi' – anyway, that's what it said in the magazine.

The Sunday Magazine

Poppy then appeared, looking rather sleepy, and wanted to know what was so interesting about the magazine that they were looking at.

They told her all about the Sumo Wrestlers. At this point all three decided it was time for breakfast and went back into the house, and also to make their human companions aware of the fallen bin.

After breakfast Sid decided to go for a walk in the neighbours garden, still thinking about Sumo wrestlers. The garden next door was very neat with its closely clipped low hedges and nicely shaped pruned trees and shrubs. However, there was one thing that was not so neat, and that was the wheelie bin that belonged to its owners. The bin, Just like his own where he had found the magazine, had fallen in the wind. Sid went to see if anything interesting had fallen out. He found a large box with a picture on the side, of a baby. But the curious thing was that the baby was wearing what appeared to him to be something that very much looked like a Sumo wrestlers mawashi

He dragged the box in his mouth to show Daisy, who he knew would be able to explain everything as she could read the lettering on the box.

Daisy had a good long study of the box and told Sid that he had picked up an unopened box of extra, extra large nappies. Sid became very excited, and said, "now I can look like the real thing - a Sumo rikishi". It was even the right size for him, and so he tried one on. And yes, he now looked the part and stood on his two back legs just like the men in the magazine and was very proud.

Sumo Cat

Later that morning whilst Sid was having a snooze after all of the excitement, Daisy started to get an idea. She thought that if she could line up a few wrestling matches on the nearby farm with some of the animals, she could then get the others to place bets on the winner. The bets could be in the form of fruit and vegetables from the farm. Daisy being a very naughty cat thought that this might also be an opportunity to secretly take some of the produce home when no one was looking.

When Sid eventually woke up Daisy explained her idea to him but left out the bit about taking some of the fruit and vegetables home.

He thought it was a good idea and that it would make him popular with the animals on the farm and he would make some new friends.

Having now put together a plan, Daisy suggested that she make a visit to Buffys Farm that was very near. In fact it could be reached across the field behind the Cottage. The two agreed that Daisy would go there early the next morning at sunrise to put her idea to the animals that were there.

Sunrise over the Farm

Chapter Two
Buffy's Farm

Daisy woke early before Sid, who had eaten an extremely large supper the night before, and was still fast asleep and snoring loudly. Poppy was also curled up on her cosy blanket near to the front door where she liked to keep an eye on all who used the cat flap during the night.

Looking out of the kitchen window and across the field towards Buffy's Farm, Daisy could see the silhouette of the farm against the red glow of the rising sun. It seemed to somehow be an omen. It reminded her of the Japanese flag, a big red circle on a white back ground which in Japanese is called Hinomaru, meaning the land of the rising sun. Daisy had read this in Sid's newly found magazine.

An early breakfast of cat biscuits and then on her way to the farm, as she was expecting a busy day ahead convincing the farm animals that the idea of organised wrestling matches with the local Sumo was going to be fun. She set off towards the farm with confidence.

There were not many animals on Farmer Buffy's farm, as he did not like animal agriculture and only did arable farming. He was quite happy growing crops and keeping the few animals that he had as pets. He would let them roam the farmyard and a large paddock to their hearts content.

As Daisy followed the slightly overgrown track next to the hedge leading to the farm, she heard the birds singing merrily. The clean smell of early spring filled the air and all seemed peaceful as the new day dawned. On approaching the farm gate Daisy could see that it was in need of repair. The hinges and latch were very old and looked to her to be very rusty. The timbers were twisted and pale.

Upon reaching the gate two figures appeared from either side looking as though they were there to ward off any unwelcome intruders who might disturb the lifestyle of the farm residents.

At the Higgely Piggely Gate

On the left there was a young, medium sized Hedgehog and from the right of the gate came a very big black Vietnamese Pot Bellied Pig, who looked very serious indeed. 'Who's that there?' asked the pig in a grumpy tone of voice. Daisy gave her name and said that she was a friend and meant no harm. She chatted to the two at the gate for some time before telling them about her friend Sid. They thought that Sid sounded the sort of Cat who would be welcome to come the farm gate and would like to meet him.

Daisy thought that this was a good time to tell them about his Wrestling. The young Hedgehog smiled, and looked cheerful but the pig had different ideas and said he would wait to see what Sid had to say for himself before he decided to let him in. What he was thinking to himself was that the idea of Wrestling matches on the farm would be big disturbance to his very well -established daily routine, which in truth did not really amount to much but it was something he knew and felt happy with.

He then had the thought that maybe if he let Daisy and Sid go ahead with this idea that he could be the first to have a wrestling match with Sid, and put him off the idea of having any more wrestling matches with any other animals. He kept this thought to himself.

Daisy said she would bring Sid to meet them at the gate but that she would like to tell Sid what their names were. The two replied almost at the same time and said that they did not have a name, and looked a bit sad. She said I shall name you Higgely the Hedgehog and Piggely the Pig. They liked this idea very much and looked very proud to be given such jolly names. Daisy then continued that she would call the farm gate the Higgely Piggely gate. This made the two feel even more important.

Daisy went back to the cottage and told the story of the two to Sid, who was now awake and had eaten an enormous breakfast. Sid was very pleased that things were on the move, that was more than could be said for him as he had eaten far too much breakfast and could hardly get through the cat flap.

When Sid had eventually managed to squeeze through, he and Daisy made their way up to the farm where the two new friends Higgely and Piggely were waiting to greet them.

After a brief introduction the gate was opened and Sid and Daisy were to be taken to see the other animals. They made their way to the large paddock where some of the farm animals had gathered to meet them. Upon entering the paddock through the large five bar wooden gate, which was secured behind them, they were approached by a jolly looking female carthorse that said, "hello my name is Paisley and you must be Daisy and Sid. Sid asked why she was called Paisley. She replied that it was because the front of her mane that came down across the top of her nose looked like the pattern paisley.

Other animals stood watching as Paisley acted as spokesperson. There was a black and white milk cow called Curly, a little hen was pacing very cautiously around the edge of the paddock, and outside the paddock gate watching very intently at what was going on were a rather snooty looking Labrador dog and an equally snooty looking Siamese cat.

Sid meets Paisley

Daisy said that she would be the chair person, as this appeared to be all but a meeting of sorts, the main and only item on the agenda being the proposed Sumo wrestling with Sid, who would be known as SumoCat.

She explained that it would be a fun idea to place bets as to who would win the wrestling matches between him and whoever fancied having a go. She also suggested that the bets could be fruit and vegetables from the farm. The animals in the paddock all agreed unanimously to go ahead with this as it looked like a lot of fun. It was now just a case of getting some volunteers to face Sid. Without hesitation Piggely was the first to say he would like to become a wrestler and was closely followed by Curly. She had always secretly wanted to be a Bull and would try to show how tough she was by making a habit of chasing anyone that came into the paddock, including the farmer who is often seen being chased. She thinks to herself that the simple-minded Sid the SumoCat will be, quite literally a push over.

The Labrador dog and the Siamese cat outside the paddock had watched and heard what was being planned. Both were unhappy about this. The Labrador whose name was James said to the cat, whose name was Shirley, that he thought the whole business was petty-minded and down-market. Shirley agreed, although her real reason for not wanting to see things go ahead was because she was very jealous of Daisy's popularity and ability to organise things.

Sid and Daisy went back home after the meeting and when they had finished supper started to think of setting a date for the first event to be held in the large paddock on the farm. Sid said he would do lots of training rolling about on the driveway at Pear Tree Cottage and grappling with the logs that were piled up near to the garage. Poppy who had now become aware of the situation, thought that the whole idea was silly, and would lead to them getting into trouble with the farmer. She decided she would not get involved but instead watch from the sidelines as her two companions made fools of themselves.

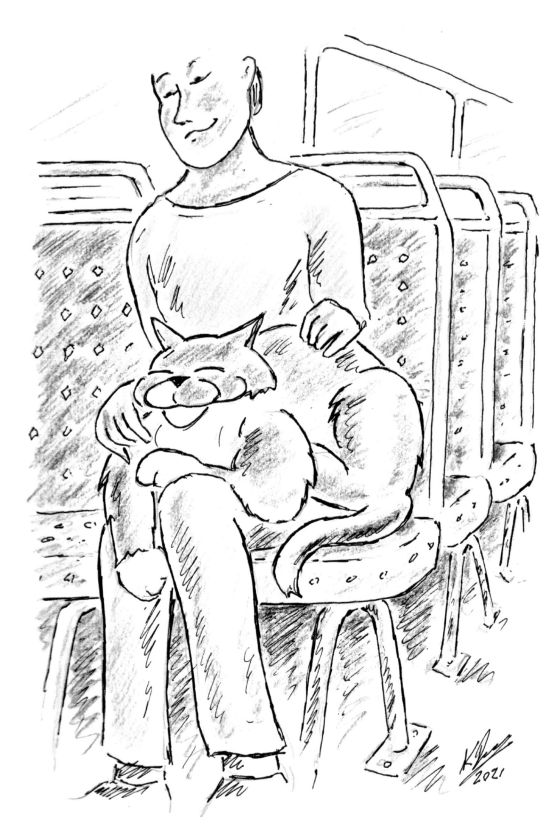

On the Way to Town

CHAPTER THREE
A TRIP INTO TOWN

It was now time to think about what the animals were to wear if they were going to have a few wrestling matches with 'SumoCat Sid'. Daisy decided that it would be a good idea to stock up with nappies. Sid still had a couple of extra, extra large ones from the packet he had found, but it would be a good idea to have at least another packet for starters.

Although Daisy thought that the nappies were a good idea, she found the whole idea of going into a chemist or supermarket to buy some a bit humiliating and beneath her. So she looked around for a suitable cuddly looking innocent to do the job. The friendly good-natured Sid appeared to fit the bill and it would keep her in control of events.

Sid sneaked onto someone's lap on a local bus and went to the nearby town. He followed a young lady with a pushchair into a shop. Daisy had previously briefed Sid what to look for when he went shopping, and had said to him, 'follow anyone with a young child who goes into a shop'.

He watched as the lady found the shelf with the nappies. Daisy has been very clever and told Sid to try and get hold of the discarded receipt for the nappies when the customer threw it away. As luck would have it, the lady accidentally dropped it and Sid quickly made a grab for it. Daisy had somehow managed to get hold of a ten-pound note and had given to it Sid before he had set off for the bus.

Sid handed the money and the receipt to the shop assistant and then pointed to the nappies on the shelf. The shop assistant understood immediately what Sid was asking for, and gave him a box of nappies and his change in a small bag. He then cheerfully caught the bus home.

When Sid arrived home with the goods Daisy showed her appreciation by giving Sid's head a good lick. Sid felt quite proud of himself and looked forward with excitement to his first wrestling match on Buffy's farm.

In the Chemist's Shop

Chapter Four
Rough and Tumble

'Let's get started' said Daisy to Sid. 'It's time to set a day and time for the first wrestling match'. Piggely, who was the first to volunteer would be SumoCat's first opponent. Daisy quickly familiarised herself with the rules of Sumo wrestling that were in the magazine article that Sid had found, and then told Sid what they were. Sid did not care too much for all this complicated stuff, and would have preferred to just get on with rolling about and looking the part. However, the rules were simple enough. It appeared that all you had to do was keep two feet on the ground and either push your opponent out of a large circle that would be marked on the ground, or topple them over.

Daisy went to the farm and made all the arrangements. The first match was to be early the next morning as soon as the farmer had gone to plough a field and his wife had gone shopping. The Farmyard would be quiet and only the animals would be there.

Sid, Daisy and Poppy made their way up to Buffy's farm early on the morning of the following day. They met Higgely and Piggely at the Higgely Piggely gate, and they all then went to the large paddock where all the animals had gathered. Sid was a bit nervous but still looking forward to his first wrestling match. By now Piggely had gone off to the far corner of the paddock and was getting himself ready. He thought it would not last very long, and that he would be the winner and put SumoCat in his place, and that would be the last of it. All could then return to normal on the farm.

The animals brought fruit and vegetables as bets. Each animal placed their items in varying amounts on the ground. Daisy had her eye on a two small cabbages that she thought would be good to attract some mice into the garden at home. She was hoping to secretly take them after the match.

The betting was simple. If you thought that SumoCat would win, you could place two items of fruit or veg. down, and if he won you would take back your fruit and also take two more items from the pile on the ground. If he lost the match then you lost your fruit. Daisy would make a note of all the bets placed by the animals.

SumoCat vs. Piggely

The paddock looked large from where SumoCat stood and in the distance, so it seemed, on the other side of the circle, that Daisy had marked out, sat Piggely. Like himself he too was dressed for the match in one of the extra, extra-large nappies and looked very serious indeed.

The crowd cheered as the two wrestlers approached each other inside the circle. Some chanted 'Come on SumoCat ' whilst other chanted 'Pigg-a-lee, Pigg-a-lee'. The two opponents bowed politely to each other and then weighed each other up before Daisy gave the start signal. Daisy raised her paw holding a little stick, and then brought it down sharply and said 'go'.

Without hesitation they grabbed each other and tried to push each other out of the circle. SumoCat decided to try and get under Piggely's great big pot belly, which totally threw the big pig off balance, as he could not move as quickly as SumoCat. This made Piggely very annoyed as he had now ended up on his back on the ground, and SumoCat was looking down at him as Daisy declared him the winner. It was all over rather quickly but apparently that was all part of Sumo wrestling.

Daisy announced to the crowd that Sumocat was now the champion and would need another challenger. Piggely was muttering and snorting loudly which everyone thought was just a pig thing to do. However he was thinking out loudly to himself that this result was now going to lead to more matches. Just at that moment Curly the cow appeared from the far corner of the paddock and was walking menacingly towards the circle. As she got closer the crowd could see that she was wearing a makeshift mawashi around her middle, which had some lettering on it.

SumoCat was now back on his spot in the circle and facing Curly. She raised herself up and squatted opposite him. The crowd could now read the lettering on the front of the mawashi, which was to be her new wrestling name 'Sue-Moo', the crowd was impressed by this dramatic entrance. Meanwhile Piggely continued muttering and snuffling. By now no one was taking much notice of the loser from the first match.

The crowd cheered again and by now SumoCat had some fans supporting him. All were starting to wonder how Sumocat could possibly overcome such a large opponent.

Daisy gave the signal and the match began. Sue-Moo poked with her nose at SumoCat, whose first instinct was to grab hold of it with his two front paws, which swept him upwards off the ground.

SumoCat wrestles with Sue-Moo

What could he do now? If she threw him down on the ground he would lose the match and he really did want to prove himself a worthy opponent of such a large challenger.

He wriggled so that he ended up covering both her eyes. Not being able to see anything and unable to shake him off of her nose, she gently lowered him to the ground so he could climb off.

The crowd clapped and cheered SumoCat who had overcome his opponent without using any force whatsoever. However the match was still not over, as one of them still needs to be pushed out of the circle or toppled over.

The signal to start was given again and this time SumoCat, thinking quickly, ran under Sue-Moo's legs as she moved towards him. That now meant that he was behind her. He put both his front paws on her and began to push hard using all his strength. The crowd chanted and encouraged him to push as hard as he could. 'I can't push any harder' he said. Sue-Moo thought that best thing to do given this situation was to sit on SumoCat and this would win her the match. Suddenly there was a loud 'Bang', which frightened all of the animals and made Su-Moo bolt out of the circle.

Farmer Buffy had returned for his lunch and seen what was going on in the paddock, and fired a shotgun into the air to stop all the nonsense. He shouted loudly 'What do you think you are a doin in that there paddock?' in a rather striking Norfolk accent. The animals ran in all directions and all but Paisley the horse and Curly the cow remained in the paddock. Farmer Buffy was really more interested in getting his lunch than wasting time with a lot of silly animals that now appeared to have disappeared for the time being, so he went into the farmhouse.

Sid, Daisy and Poppy went home. Daisy said to the other two that she felt that the day had been a success, as SumoCat had now become the hero of the day, even though the Farmer had interrupted the last match. She then remembered all the fruit and vegetables that had been piled up as bets and said 'Oh dear I do hope that the animals on the farm put them out of the way so that Farmer Buffy does not see them'. Sid said that he was very pleased by the way that things had turned out but was very tired and hungry. Poppy said that she was not surprised that the farmer had got upset, and that they were very lucky that he liked animals and was more interested in having his lunch.

Chapter Five
The Little Visitor

Two days had passed since the events on the farm. Sid was still as enthusiastic as ever and keen to train to keep himself fit for his next adventure as SumoCat. He was sure that Daisy would eventually come up with another idea now, being his manager.

He made very sure that his human domestics provided lots of food in order to maintain his figure, as a Sumo should. He did this by making a lot of noise in the kitchen, especially when the humans were near and preparing their own food. If they didn't take much notice of him he would start to rearrange the kitchen by practising his Sumo moves on a few saucepans. This made a lot of noise and always did the job.

He trained hard in the driveway by tossing logs around; the bigger the better he thought as this would prepare him for large opponents.

On this particular morning whilst grabbing and throwing a medium sized log across the drive, just for starters, he had a rather prickly experience. Not really concentrating he pounced, as best he could, onto what he thought was the log he had just thrown which had landed on some grass in the shade of a tree next to the drive. He was startled as he landed to find that it was very sharp and prickly and started to move. Daisy and Poppy were nearby and heard him make a loud meow. They ran to see what was wrong. By the time they got to him, he was sitting in the driveway next to a medium sized hedgehog. As soon as the hedgehog looked at them they knew immediately who he was: it was Higgely from the farm.

'That's a nice way to greet your new friend' said Higgely to Sid. Sid replied that had mistaken Higgely for his training log. Sid sounded very concerned that he had upset his new friend, and so invited him into the house for some cat biscuits.

The three cats and the hedgehog went into the house and had some lunch together in the kitchen. Higgely said that things on the farm had not been the same since the wrestling match, and the animals on the farm had all agreed that it was great fun and wanted to do it again, and also they were missing their three new friends from Pear Tree Cottage. Higgely said that he had offered to come down into the village and seek out Sid, Daisy and Poppy.

The Little Visitor

As the four were chatting away they could hear the sound of a tractor busy in the field behind the cottage. Poppy jumped up onto the kitchen sink so that she could see what was going on out of the window. It was a large field and it looked as though Farmer Buffy was going to be ploughing it for the rest of the day at least. She said to Higgely 'I think it best that you stay here until the morning before making your way back to the farm as it could be dangerous to walk up the footpath next to the hedge in the field'. Higgely agreed to stay. Sid said there was plenty of food and there was always a bowl of water and some biscuits available for snacking.

It was nice to have a guest stay, said Poppy and Sid thought that he now had someone around to show off his new found tumbling skills to in the driveway.

It was a warm sunny afternoon in the garden following lunch. Higgely explained that the animals on the farm were so impressed by SumoCat that some of them were also practicing, pushing large stones around and seeing if they could keep upright on two legs and not lose their balance. This made Sid feel very important indeed. Daisy was also very pleased that her idea had worked. Poppy was happy that so far they had all managed to stay out of trouble, but was still a bit concerned that this was still a recipe for things to go wrong if Daisy did not manage them properly. She was sure that the farmer must have noticed that there were some strange things starting to happen on the farm.

The three cats made Higgely very welcome. They made him a nice bed to sleep in under an old Windsor chair in a quiet corner of the dining room, away from the cat flap which could sometimes be very noisy during the night as there were sometimes a lot of comings and goings, not to mention the wind blowing it open from time to time.

Daisy said to Higgely 'You must tell them on the farm that we will have a return match as soon as possible'. Higgely asked if he could tell them when it would be. Daisy replied 'I think the day after tomorrow would be good'. She had looked at the weather forecast earlier and it looked as though there would be no rain for the rest of that week.

All was quiet now in the house and the friends settled down for the
night feeling quite pleased with themselves.

The Stop Over

CHAPTER SIX
TOPKNOTS

The day had arrived for SumoCat to face his opponents in the large paddock on Buffy's farm. A re-match was planned with Sue-Moo and then, anyone who wanted to join in the fun.

They all gathered around the circle, as before, and the animals that lived on the farm were glad to see their friends from the village. By now the animals in support of their wrestling heroes were wearing topknots on their heads. These were regularly worn as part of the Sumo wrestlers outfits, and called a chonmage. But just to add a special touch, it was agreed that the contestants would have different coloured topknots so that the supporters of each one could wear a similar one showing which one was their hero.

SumoCat wore a bright red chonmage. His hair was not long enough to tie into a knot on the top of his head, so Daisy had made him one out of piece of material held on with an elastic band, which went around his head and under his chin. She let the other contestants wear whatever colour they decided was appropriate. Both she and Poppy wore a similar one to SumoCat.

They all placed their bets and put their fruit and vegetables in a pile. Once again Daisy made a note of the bets made by each animal. There was a much bigger pile than the first time, and Daisy thought that this looked very encouraging.

It was a Japanese tradition for each contestant to throw some salt into the circle before each match for purification. Daisy had read up about this as she wanted to get things right. Sid thought that it was so they did not slip over when they were wrestling but he was still happy to do as Daisy said.

The first to challenge SumoCat to a re-match was Sue-Moo who was sporting a bright blue topknot. Both threw some salt into the circle and then squatted on their marked out positions in the circle. Both front feet were to be placed on the ground in front of them before they were to start. This made the pair look very professional. It looked just like the two men Sid had seen in the Magazine.

Top Knots

Daisy then raised her stick and brought it down sharply. The crowd cheered loudly as SumoCat without hesitation-grabbed hold of one of Sue-Moo's back legs. She tried in vain to shake him off. By now SumoCat had made himself very strong after training on all of those logs and was not going to let go. He made sure that he did not take his back feet off the ground as Sue-Moo starting spinning around in circles to try and make him let go. This went on for some time and Sue-Moo was getting very dizzy. She thought that if she changed direction and spun in the other direction it might do the trick. This was not a good idea. When she stopped suddenly and tried to go the other way she fell over onto her side. SumoCat was still clinging to her back leg and had still managed to keep his own back paws on the ground. A great cheer went up from the crowd, as once again SumoCat was the winner. He was now the undefeated champion.

Piggely was still nursing his wounds from the previous match that he had with SumoCat, and was still sulking. He was not ready for a second humiliation just yet so he kept out of the way, but watched from near the edge of the paddock. As he sat there he could see the Labrador dog and the Siamese cat watching from outside the paddock. They looked very serious and were not having any part of the activities. Although Piggely was feeling sorry for himself, he was not a bad natured animal, and had by now become a secret admirer of SumoCat Sid and liked him. He would never wish him harm, and felt that something was wrong with the way that the Labrador and the Siamese cat were behaving.

Meanwhile back in the middle of the paddock there was a lot of commotion and Daisy was sorting out the bets before they had any interruptions, remembering what happened the last time they were there. The animals wearing the bright red topknots gathered their winnings.

Once all the animals had cleared up all the fruit and vegetables Daisy stood in the circle and called for another volunteer to challenge SumoCat, but nobody came forward. The animals needed time to consider, as it was obvious they were now dealing with a professional.

Daisy said she thought that they had all had enough fun for one day and that when they decided upon another challenger they should let her know. It was agreed that Higgely would come down to the cottage as soon as the farm animals had found a worthy opponent.

As the sun dipped towards the horizon in the late evening that day, the three cats who were by now relaxing in their garden at Pear Tree Cottage, felt satisfied that the days ahead would be full of surprises.

Up to No Good

Chapter Seven

The Tempest

Several very hot, sunny days had passed since Sid, Daisy and Poppy had seen their friends on the farm. It had been far too hot to even think about wrestling matches in the large paddock, especially for a very large black and white cat like Sid. Even SumoCat needed to take a break from rolling about in the sun.

It was late one evening when Sid said to Daisy 'I am sure that I can hear strange rumbling noises outside'. Both cats knew that on this occasion it was not Sid's stomach making the noises.

Poppy too was feeling a bit concerned, and the three of them went to the cat flap to look outside through the transparent plastic flap panel. In the distance they saw a zigzag of light come from a very dark cloud and a loud bang followed. It frightened them so much they all retreated to the kitchen. Sid was very worried about their friends on the farm. He said 'We really must try and get to them in case they need our help and the zigzags from the sky come down on the farm. Daisy and Poppy agreed, but were a bit scared to go out into the night with all that noise from the sky going on. Sid said he would have to go whatever happened. So, without having a concern for his own safety, he wriggled through the cat flap and bravely made his way through the rain amidst the rumblings. He felt very nervous, as he did not know when the next big bang would happen, although he remembered that the last one came just after the big zigzag of light.

He arrived at the Higgely Piggely gate and there was no sign of his two friends who would normally be there. He crawled under the gate and made his way to the large paddock. It was the only part of the farm that he knew, and he was sure that he would find Curly the cow and Paisley the carthorse there. Sure enough, upon reaching the paddock, he saw that they were running around and looking scared of all the noise. He jumped up and released the catch on the gate to the paddock and the gate swung open. Both Curly and Paisley did not hesitate to dash out and head towards a large barn that was nearby, closely followed by Sid.

Into the barn they ran, only just ahead of a flash and bang from above. It sounded so loud and happened so suddenly, that it made poor Sid jump through the air and do quite a spectacular summersault into the barn.

The Tempest

There was only one problem: he had somehow managed to land on Paisley's back. He stood up and realised that he was staring into her great big eyes and it startled him so much that he fell down near to her front hooves.

Looking up he could see that she was smiling at him. She said 'Do not be afraid you are my little Hero'. This made him feel quite special and put him at his ease. It was nice to be a little hero as well as a big Sumo he thought, especially as Paisley was so big herself, and could quite easily be a big challenge as a wrestling opponent. She said 'Here at the farm you can always feel at home with your friends, and should never need be afraid that anyone would want to hurt you'. This was very true of most of the animals on the farm. However, there was still a very real danger lurking that Sid and most of the animals were not aware of. The rather uppity Labrador James, and the equally snooty Siamese cat Shirley, were secretly plotting to find a way of stopping the wrestling matches.

As Sid's eyes became adjusted to the light in the barn he could see the other animals from the farm had also taken shelter there. There was Higgely and Piggely sitting together near a bale of straw, Mildred the hen was strutting about looking grumpy as usual and by now Curly the cow had found something to munch on. She was chewing away at grass near to the barn door. They all waited patiently for the storm to pass, although it did look as though it would go on for some time.

Paisley could see something shiny just poking out from a rather untidy looking bale of straw and went to investigate. It was the farmer's radio that he had forgotten, and left lying in the barn. She said to Sid 'It would be fun to pass the time with some music if you could use your paw to switch it on'. Sid had a go and pushed what he thought was the right button on the top of the radio. Sure enough he was right first time, as luck would have it, and music came loud and clear from the radio's speaker. It was a strange kind of music that had a strong beat, and looking up at all the other animals he could see that they were all swaying with the rhythm. He also felt as though he wanted to move to the sound, so he started to sway himself. Now he thought 'What if we made up a few dance moves to go with the music?'. He jumped up and started kicking his legs out; left, left, right, right, left, left, left, right,

right, right and then jumped around so his back was facing them. He then jumped around to face them and could see that they had all lined up and were copying him. He shouted above the sound of the music 'This is the dance we can do before our wrestling contests; it can be the Rikishi shuffle'. He had remembered that the word for wrestler in Japanese was Rikishi.

The Labrador and the Siamese cat watched from near the barn door. James said to Shirley 'Here is our opportunity to make the farmer do something about all this nonsense'.

In the Barn

Shirley nodded in agreement. Shirley replied 'Go and bark loudly under the farmers bedroom window and wake him, if he had not already been woken by the noise from the barn'.

James went to the farmhouse and started barking and howling under the window that he knew was the farmer's bedroom.

The farmer lifted the sash window and looked out bleary-eyed. He was wearing a striped nightshirt and cap and looked very old fashioned. He heard the noise coming from the barn, muttered to himself, and looked annoyed. The window was shut with a loud thump. And moments later he came rushing out of the house with his shotgun. 'These animals are out of control and becoming a nuisance', he thought to himself, and something had to be done.

James ran ahead and arrived at the barn first. He then stood outside and started barking. The farmer went into the barn in a rage waving his shotgun as though he was about to use it. Just as he appeared at the entrance of the barn, there was a loud thunderclap from the sky, at the same time the whole sky seemed to light up like daylight. This made the farmer appear as a dark silhouette in the barn entrance. The animals scattered in fright to the far corners of the barn and some hid behind the bales of straw.

The farmer turned the radio off with the butt of his gun and looked very angry. He shouted 'If you lot can't behave proper you will have to be kept separate from each other', in his usual Norfolk accent.

James and Shirley grinned smugly from afar feeling rather pleased with themselves.

Sid made his way home as the storm had now eased. Being summer, the soft glow on the horizon told him that he had been out all night and it definitely was time to get some sleep. He had much to tell his two companions at Pear Tree Cottage, but that would have to wait until after he had rested. He felt sad that after having such a good time with his friends on the farm it should end in such a bad way with the farmer getting upset. He thought that maybe if Daisy had been with him she would have known why the farmer had been so angry.

Back at the farm there was one who did understand what was going on. Piggely who had been keeping his eye on James and Shirley knew exactly what they were up to.

Farmer Buffy Appears

At the earliest opportunity Piggely was going to let his friends at Pear Tree Cottage know the facts. He spoke to his companion Higgely and told him that he would need to go down to the village and see Sid, Daisy and Poppy and explain what had happened, and that James and Shirley had gone and woken the farmer.

Chapter Eight
Rescued

It was midday and Sid was lying on his back on the driveway of Pear Tree Cottage basking in the sunlight. It was very peaceful, and the only sounds were the birdsong and Sid snoring. Daisy and Poppy were in the garden. Daisy was upsetting one of the birds that she thought was making far too much noise. She then heard Sid snoring and thought he too should have a good telling off. As she strode purposefully towards him, Higgely appeared in the driveway looking rather dusty from the dry soil that he had been disturbed as he came down the track from the farm.

He shook the dust from his back and said good afternoon to his friends. Sid gave a very loud snore and woke up with a start. He must have been dreaming about wrestling because as soon as he woke he jumped up and squatted with his front paws on the ground as if he was ready for a match. He then realised he was looking at Daisy and Higgely, and smiled.

Higgely told them about the Labrador dog and Siamese cat and that they had woken the farmer the previous night, otherwise he would not have heard the music in the barn above the sound of the storm, which he appeared to be sleeping through. 'So that was what you were all doing on the farm last night' said Daisy.

Sid said 'Lets have another wrestling match up on the farm, and this time make sure that the Labrador dog is my next opponent'. Daisy said to Sid 'You must not have a wrestling match with anyone you feel annoyed with'. She was confident that the dog and cat on the farm would eventually get themselves in a muddle if they carried on behaving badly.

Daisy suggested they all go up to the farm and try to calm things down, as she didn't want this to stop them from having future wrestling matches. Higgely then said 'The farmer was so upset that he had now

43

put a padlock on the large paddock gate so that Curly and Paisley could not get out'. Sid became very annoyed and said 'What if we have another storm and they cannot take shelter in the barn. Something will have to be done'. Higgely then told him that the farmer had also locked the barn door by using a large sliding bolt made of wood. This made Sid even angrier. Daisy told him to calm down and that this situation needed some thought before they went up to the farm. They all thought that this was a sensible suggestion, and sat together to think about what to do. Poppy came and joined them.

Snoring Loudly

After much consideration they all agreed that the best thing to do would be for Sid, Daisy and Poppy to apologise to the farmer properly, and take him a nice bunch of wild flowers. Daisy could write out a letter. Farmer Buffy was a kindly man and although he had become annoyed with the animals, they were sure he would unlock the Paddock and unbolt the barn if he was told properly what had been going on with the wrestling matches. They could even invite him and his wife to come and watch.

Daisy said 'I will write a letter first thing tomorrow morning. I am certain that there is a pencil or pen in one of the small pots on the table in the sitting room, and I most certainly could find some paper to write on'.

They were all happy with this idea, although Sid was still worried about his friends being locked up and could not get to sleep that night for thinking of them.

He decided enough was enough, he had to rescue his friends from captivity. The best thing to do, he thought, would be to dress in his Mawashi and pull his headband that he wore for wrestling matches down over his eyes. He made two slits in the headband so that he could see. This would make him feel as though he was on a rescue mission and make him easily recognisable to the animals on the farm in the dark.

Off to the farm he went, through the now unattended Higgely Piggely gate and towards the paddock. When he arrived he told Curly and Paisley to be very quiet, so as to not wake the farmer or his wife.

His first thought was to jump up onto the paddock fence so that he could speak in a whisper to his friends. Up he went and grabbed the top rail of the fence. 'Ker-ack!' went the wooden rail that was rotten and had snapped under Sid's weight. Sid had now fallen backwards, and was lying on his back looking up at the two prisoners. He said to them 'The fence is now low enough for you both to jump over'. Over they went, and the three then quietly walked towards the barn where their other friends had been locked in.

46

As they reached the barn, they could see the long wooden bar that was holding the door shut. Sid told Paisley to raise her front hoof and knock it sideways and see if she could release it. She gave the end of the bar a good kick that loosened it. Another, and it went flying and landed with a loud clatter on the stable block paving near the barn entrance. The barn door suddenly flew open with Piggely being the first to appear. He had heard them outside trying to open the door, and as soon as the bolt had been knocked out had given it an almighty push.

Mildred Makes a Noise

Mildred the hen came out flapping her wings, squawking and making a terrible racket. It was impossible to get her to calm down, and the lights had come on in the farmhouse. Sid said 'The only thing we can do is run away'. They all ran to the Higgely Piggely gate. As they came close to the gate with the farmer chasing them, closely followed by James the Labrador, Sid tripped on a large flint stone, as he was looking back and not at where he was going. 'Bonk!' He banged his head on the gatepost and became very dizzy; he could just see the farmer getting closer as everything seemed to go dark.

He woke with Daisy shaking him saying 'Wake up you great big lazy old SumoCat, this won't win you any wrestling matches'. For a moment he was very confused. Where was he? The last thing he remembered was being near the gate on the farm. Then he realised what had happened. He had fallen asleep whilst thinking about his friends on the farm and had been dreaming.

Sid said 'What are we going to do now?' Daisy told him that while he was asleep, she and Poppy had been up to the farm and seen Mr Buffy. She had taken him some wild flowers and handed him a note as they had agreed the night before. After reading the note that explained that they were sorry for waking him up, she told him about the organised wrestling matches, he had smiled and forgiven them. He also had said that he would like Sid, Daisy and Poppy to come to the farm as his guests and organise a big display-wrestling match, and that he would provide lots of food for the event. He also added that, as it was to be held during the day, they could also make use of his music player. So, it was not a radio but a music player that they had found in the barn. This was very good news as it meant that the tune that they had all been dancing to was a recording, and could be played whenever they wanted to do their Rikishi shuffle dance before a match. Poppy said that she had thanked the farmer for being so kind, and that they would accept his invitation.

As it looked like being a big event, she had also asked the farmer if they could put up some notices telling all about it so that anyone interested could come and watch. He agreed to this and said he would help them to put some up in the village.

Sid had much to think about now. He would need to do a lot of training, and wanted to give a good show for his supporters and any new spectators that would be there. There was no time to lose.

CHAPTER NINE
THE SUR-PRIZE FIGHTER

It was the night before the big wrestling event on the farm and Sid was hoping for a good night's sleep so that he would be ready for any new challengers that may lie ahead.

One thing was playing on his mind, however, and proving to be a bit of a distraction. The large food bowl that was placed outside the front door of the cottage was always empty in the mornings. The bowl of food, he thought, must be there for any night visitors who may not have a home, and are hungry with no human domestics to care for them. Higgely had admitted to him that occasionally when visiting Pear Tree Cottage and no one was around, he would have a nibble if there were food in the bowl. But on this occasion there appeared to be some ginger fur near the bowl.

He thought no more of it, as there were far more important things to think about. All the preparations had been made for the event on the farm. Little posters had been put up on gates at the end of cottage gardens and on telegraph poles in the village and also one had been placed on the village notice board.

Sid, Daisy and Poppy had all had a good night's sleep, and were up early the next morning and ready for the day ahead and feeling quite exited. They had breakfast and all ventured up to the Higgely Piggely gate. When they got there a crowd was there to greet them. It was a much bigger crowd than any of the three cats had expected, and it made Sid feel even more nervous realising that there was going to be a lot of eyes watching him in the circle. He said to Daisy ' I think that I have butterflies in my tummy'. Daisy replied 'Well that's the best place for them, don't let any of your opponents know they are there'.

When they arrived at the large paddock, the farmer was there to greet them. A pile of hay bales had been arranged for Daisy to stand on so that everyone who was there could see her. A microphone had also been placed there. Paisley said to Daisy 'Climb onto my nose and I will lift you up onto the bales of hay'. Without hesitating, Daisy climbed onto her nose and Paisley put her on the top bale. As she did so she heard the sound of the music that they had danced to in the barn being played.

Daisy Makes an Announcement

The crowd were cheering but no one was dancing at this stage. 'I guess that this will happen later', she thought to herself.

Farmer Buffy made the first announcements. He welcomed everyone to his farm for the event, and introduced Daisy. He then placed the microphone on the stand for Daisy to speak. She told the crowd that the first two bouts would be between three contestants; SumoCat, Sue-Moo and Piggely, and asked them to place their bets in the usual manner.

She then climbed back onto Paisleys nose and was lowered to the ground. Daisy took up her place in the circle and raised her stick for the first match between SumoCat and Sue-Moo.

All of the bouts had been carefully planned, and for the sake of making this a very entertaining event, they had rehearsed some rather spectacular tumbles and shuffles. This made clouds of dust as they crashed and rolled about in the circle. Then Piggely joined in the fun and as the morning progressed, there was an even number of wins between them.

It was now time for a tea break and food and drinks were available in abundance. The farmer was a good as his word and had refreshments laid on for all present.

Following a well-earned break, SumoCat was refreshed and ready for any new challengers. Daisy went back up to the microphone and called for a new challenger to come forward.

A loud cheer went up, and to everyone's surprise, there was a new opponent appearing.

There was a row of animals, mainly stray cats that had lined up at one end of the paddock, looking as though they were hiding something behind them. All went silent for a moment. And then they began chanting loudly, 'Jinja-Tom, Jinja-Tom, Jinja-Tom. The line parted in the middle and forward came a rather large Ginger Cat looking very much like a Ginger version of SumoCat. This made Sid very nervous indeed and his butterflies returned, only this time they felt like a flock of starlings fluttering about.

This was going to be a totally unrehearsed bout, and SumoCat would have to tackle this unknown opponent without having any idea of what he was like.

SumoCat Vs. Jinja-Tom

By now Daisy was back in the circle and ready with her stick raised. The two wrestlers crouched and stared at each other. Meanwhile the crowd were cheering them on, as bets were being placed frantically in a sort of half organised pile, and poor Poppy trying to make a hurried note of them. As before, all of the supporters wore a coloured topknot in the colour of their hero, and the Jinja-Tom supporters wore bright orange ones.

Daisy gave the signal to start and the two wrestlers grabbed each other's Mawashi's. They shuffled around first to the right, and then to the left, and for a while it looked as though neither were going to win. It looked very much like a new dance, which certainly would go with the music on the farmer's music player. They then swayed to the left and both were hopping on one foot, and then the same to the right. It looked so funny that the crowd began laughing and cheering at the same time. Suddenly without warning their dance tune was being played over the loud speakers that were meant for the microphone. The crowd all began to pair off and grab each other similar to the wrestlers and began copying their movements to the rhythm of the music. By now the wrestlers had become totally distracted by this and had joined in the dancing. Remembering the other moves that they done in the barn to the music, Sid managed to get some of the animals to form a line and do the kicking routine. The other animals copied them, and by alternating the kicking bit with the bit where they circled around with a partner, they put together a proper dance routine. All the animals were having a good time and enjoying themselves immensely.

They danced for some time until the farmer announced on the microphone that he felt it was time for everyone to have a sit down. He said, 'I think you lot had better sit yourselves down and have a rest afore you all fall down'. They all did as the farmer had suggested and sat own and caught their breath.

As Sid sat on the ground with his new friend Jinja-Tom, he asked him where he had come from. Tom replied 'I have been a visitor to Pear Tree Cottage for some time, but I only come during the night when it's quiet, to eat at the food bowl outside the cottage door'. Now Sid knew exactly who the mystery visitor was and was glad to meet him. Tom Explained that he was a stray, and did not have a home Like Sid, Daisy and Poppy, and hoped that they did not mind if he came and ate from the bowl at night. Daisy and Poppy came over and joined them and Sid told them what Tom had just said. They said to Tom that they were happy for him to come to the cottage whenever he wanted to, and would like to see him at any time. They did not want him to feel lonely and told him that he would always have a home in the garden of Pear Tree Cottage.

Dancing in the Paddock

They were pretty sure that their human domestics would also be happy with this arrangement, as they were very fond of cats. This would also mean that Sid would have a sparring partner who he could train with and they could practice all sorts of spectacular moves for future events. Tom thought this was a good idea.

The Day gently settled into evening and the four cats, including Tom of course, went back to Pear Tree Cottage and spent a quiet and relaxing time after supper in the garden.

Back at the farm the farmer was clearing up after the event and felt pleased that all the animals had enjoyed the day. His wife, who had been quietly watching, was happy to see her husband and all the animals having such a good time.

It was obvious to everyone including Farmer Buffy, that SumoCat was going to be a big celebrity; but that's another story.

A Time to Relax

Printed in Great Britain
by Amazon

38918624R00044